My Secret Alien

Elizabeth Dale

Illustrated by Steven Wood

Green Bananas

EGMONT
We bring stories to life

Book Band: Orange

First published in Great Britain 2013
by Egmont UK Ltd
The Yellow Building, 1 Nicholas Road, London W11 4AN
Text copyright © Elizabeth Dale 2013
Illustrations copyright © Steven Wood 2013
The author and illustrator have asserted their moral rights.
ISBN 978 1 4052 5945 3
10 9 8 7 6 5 4 3 2 1
A CIP catalogue record for this title is available from the British Library.
Printed in Singapore.
49137/1

EGMONT LUCKY COIN

Our story began over a century ago, when seventeen-year-old Egmont Harald Petersen found a coin in the street.

He was on his way to buy a flyswatter, a small hand-operated printing machine that he then set up in his tiny apartment.

The coin brought him such good luck that today Egmont has offices in over 30 countries around the world. And that lucky coin is still kept at the company's head offices in Denmark.

A New Friend for Charlie

Happy Birthday, Charlie!

Zak at the Seaside

For Austin,
who has almost super
alien fixing powers!
E.D.

For Sam,
who pretends not to notice
when I eat all the biscuits
S.W.

A New Friend for Charlie

Charlie was playing when he felt
something wriggling in his pocket.
Was it a spider? A worm? Worse?

'Hello!' it called.

Charlie jumped. 'Who are you?' he

cried.

I'm Zak!

'What are you doing in my pocket?'

asked Charlie.

'It's the best place!' said Zak. 'It's full of tasty munch-magic! We only eat protein-pods on Zog.'

'Zog?' Charlie cried. 'You're an alien? Wow! Magic!'

Brilliant!

'I'm exploring earth,' said Zak.

'You're my special earth-friend.

Only you can see me.'

Zak loved Charlie's house. 'We don't have bouncy chairs on Zog!' he said.

'Or swings inside . . .'

'. . . or so many pretty things.'

But Charlie's bedroom was the best.

'Brilliant toys!' Zak cried.

'That's my train,' said Charlie.

'It's broken.'

'Soon fix that!' said Zak. 'We

Zoggians are techno-wizards.'

Zak fixed it so well, the train zoomed

up the wall and across the ceiling!

15

'Mum's coming back!' said Charlie.

'Everywhere's a mess!'

'Don't worry, I'm a time traveller!'

said Zak. 'Hold my hand. We'll

travel back to when I arrived.'

WHOOSH!!!

Suddenly Charlie was downstairs.

'That was brilliant!' he cried.

But Zak had gone.

'I'm back in your pocket!' said Zak.

'It's my favourite place!'

Happy Birthday, Charlie!

Charlie was very excited. It was his birthday and all his friends were coming to his party.

Zak was excited, too. All that

party food looked delicious!

21

Zak tasted the birthday cake and
splodged in the trifle.

Then he jumped into the ice cream.

That was a mistake!

F-f-f-freezing!

Soon Charlie's friends arrived.

Zak watched them from Charlie's

pocket . . .

. . . though sometimes it was difficult

to stay there!

Suddenly there was a clap of thunder.

Everyone jumped – even more than

they were jumping already!

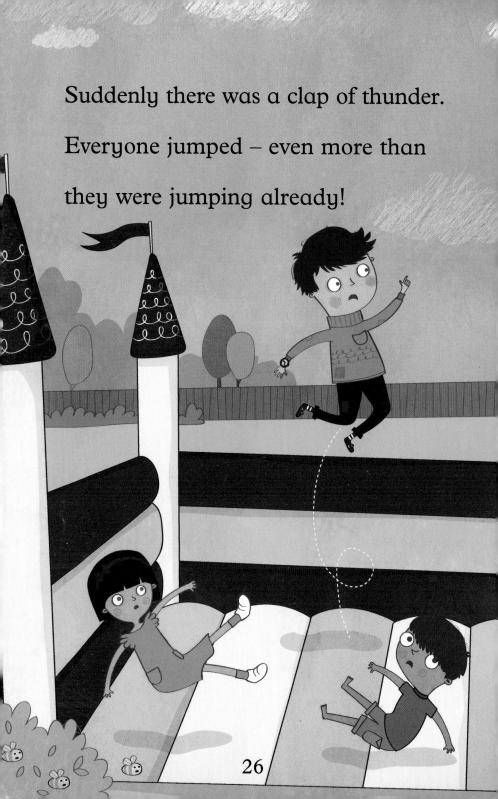

Charlie looked up. It was going to rain. They wouldn't be able to play outside or bounce any more.

No!

CLAP! Flash!

Charlie peered into his pocket.

Zak wasn't there!

Don't be frightened, Zak!

Charlie looked around. Was Zak

hiding because he was scared?

'Charlie!' called his mum.

But Charlie had to find Zak.

Come in, quick!

Suddenly the sun came out.

It was wonderful.

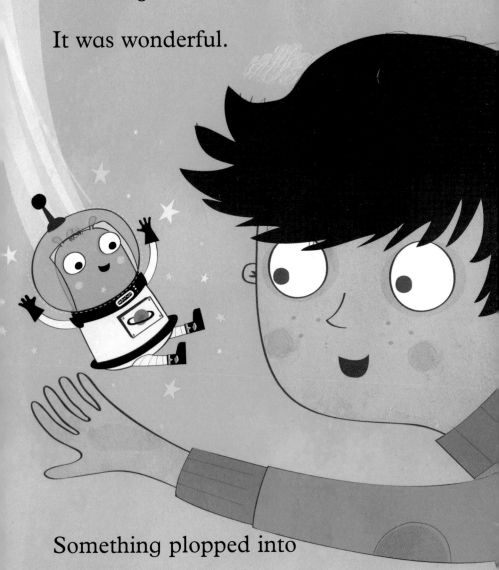

Something plopped into

Charlie's hand.

'I've been flying through the clouds to break them up!' said Zak. 'Come on, let's get bouncing!'

Zak at the Seaside

Charlie was so excited. He was
going to the seaside for the day.

34

'Cool!' cried Zak when he

saw the waves.

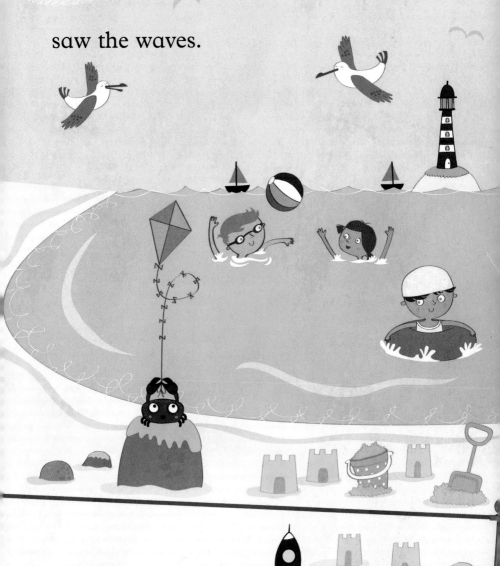

Zak loved surfing on the sea . . .

until a really big wave came.

On the beach, they found pretty

shells and friendly crabs.

Then Charlie had an ice cream.

'Don't like that!' said Zak. 'Too

cold!'

But Zak tried some anyway –

and loved it!

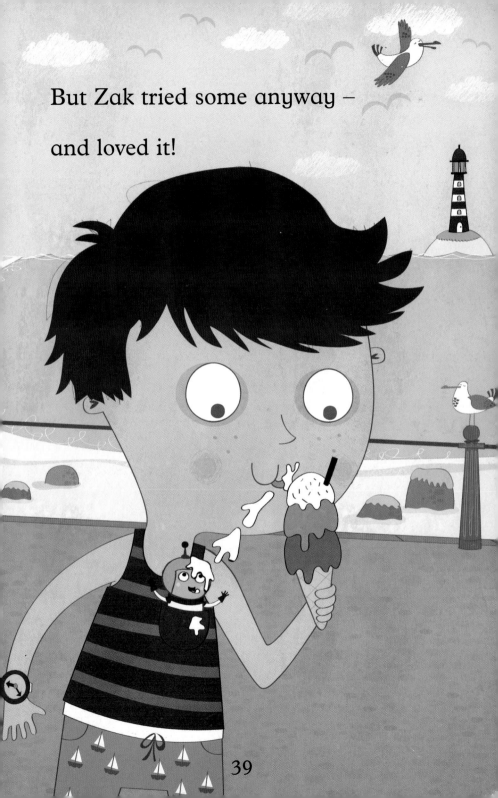

Suddenly Charlie discovered that

his new watch was missing.

'It's fallen into the sand!' he cried.

'It's lost forever.'

Zak's alien magnetic fingers found
coins, rings . . . and finally Charlie's
watch.

'Let's go for a swim!' Charlie

suggested.

'Too scary!' said Zak.

Charlie had fun swimming, but
he missed Zak. So he ran back
to his friend.

But Zak just lay in Charlie's pocket.

'I'm poorly,' he said. 'I've eaten too

much earth food. I must go home.'

Charlie was so sad

to see Zak go.

45

How Charlie missed his friend.

He couldn't sleep that night.

The next morning he was

woken by something bouncy!

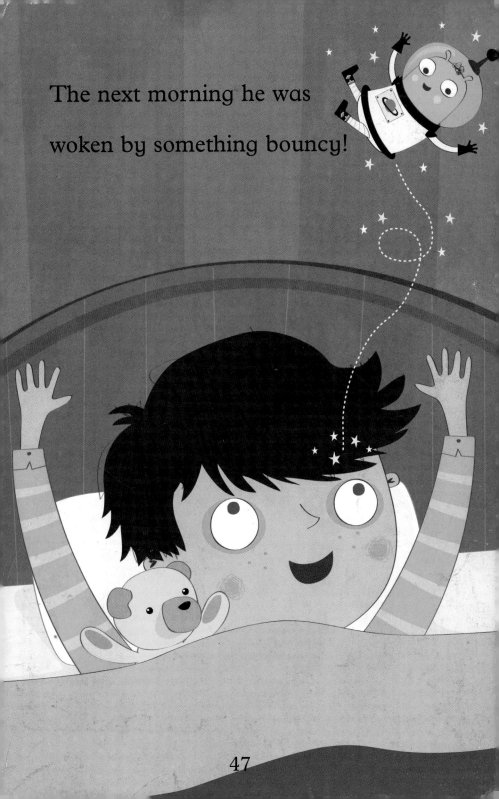

'You don't get rid of me that easily!' said Zak. 'As long as I can keep popping home for food, I'll always be around.'

Charlie grinned.

They were friends forever!